# Run!

First published in 2002 by
Franklin Watts
338 Euston Road
London
NW1 3BH

Franklin Watts Australia
Level 17/207 Kent Street
Sydney
NSW 2000

A CIP catalogue record for this book is available
from the British Library.

ISBN 978 0 7496 4705 6

**Series Editor:** Jackie Hamley
**Series Advisor:** Dr Barrie Wade
**Cover Design:** Jason Anscomb
**Design:** Peter Scoulding

Printed in China

Franklin Watts is a division of
Hachette Children's Books,
an Hachette Livre UK company
www.hachettelivre.co.uk

For my mother
– SF

# Run!

by Sue Ferraby and Fabiano Fiorin

W
FRANKLIN WATTS
LONDON•SYDNEY

Once a mouse called Jimjon
left his home in the rustling
leaves of the Tangly Wood.
He went night-visiting.

He crept under the tight fence
and through a grass stalk tunnel
to a little house.

Jimjon climbed the
cold stone steps.

He squeezed under the door.
He tiptoed over the prickly mat
into the kitchen.

All night long he ate crumbs in
the shadows under the stairs.

By and by the stars went pale.
The moon set. "I must get home
before the sun comes up,"
thought Jimjon.

Out of the shadows under
the stairs, Jimjon ran.

But a cat sat on the prickly mat.

So Jimjon couldn't get home.

Jimjon stopped. He listened.
He looked.

Jimjon saw that the cat was really
a coat, dropped in a heap.

Out of the shadows under
the stairs, across the prickly
mat, Jimjon ran.

But a giant stood on the cold stone
steps, guarding the door. Jimjon
couldn't get home.

Jimjon stopped. He listened.
He looked.

He saw that the giant feet were
not feet at all, but a pair of big
boots left outside.

Out of the shadows under the
stairs, across the prickly mat, down
the cold stone steps, Jimjon ran.

But a ghost spread its hands over the grass stalk tunnel, so Jimjon couldn't get home.

Jimjon stopped. He listened.

He looked.

He saw that the ghost was a piece
of paper, flapping in the wind.

Out of the shadows under the stairs, across the prickly mat, down the cold stone steps, through the grass stalk tunnel, Jimjon ran.

But an owl sat near the tight
fence, watching even the smallest
thing that moved.

Jimjon stopped. He listened.
He looked.

The owl looked straight back at
him. Jimjon's heart froze with fear.

Then Jimjon saw that the owl was
the great sun rising through the
branches of the Tangly Wood.
It was morning.

Out of the shadows under the stairs, across the prickly mat, down the cold stone steps, through the grass stalk tunnel and under the tight fence, Jimjon ran.

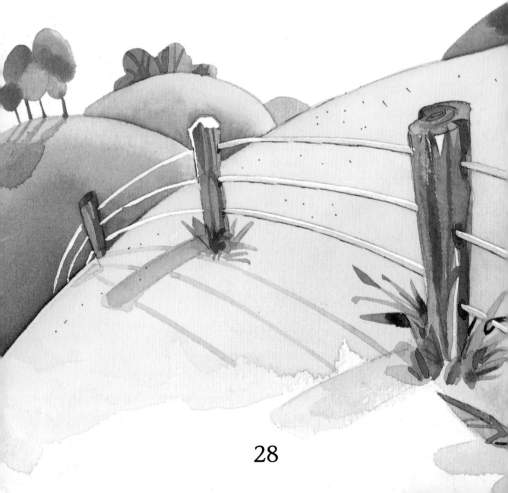

Home he ran, to the rustling leaves of the Tangly Wood, where he was...

...safe at last.

**Hopscotch has been specially designed to fit the requirements of the Literacy Framework. It offers real books by top authors and illustrators for children developing their reading skills.**

**Marvin, the Blue Pig**
ISBN 978 0 7496 4619 6

**Plip and Plop**
ISBN 978 0 7496 4620 2

**The Queen's Dragon**
ISBN 978 0 7496 4618 9

**Flora McQuack**
ISBN 978 0 7496 4621 9

**Willie the Whale**
ISBN 978 0 7496 4623 3

**Naughty Nancy**
ISBN 978 0 7496 4622 6

**Run!**
ISBN 978 0 7496 4705 6

**The Playground Snake**
ISBN 978 0 7496 4706 3

**"Sausages!"**
ISBN 978 0 7496 4707 0

**Bear in Town**
ISBN 978 0 7496 5875 5

**Pippin's Big Jump**
ISBN 978 0 7496 4710 0

**Whose Birthday Is It?**
ISBN 978 0 7496 4709 4

**The Princess and the Frog**
ISBN 978 0 7496 5129 9

**Flynn Flies High**
ISBN 978 0 7496 5130 5

**Clever Cat**
ISBN 978 0 7496 5131 2

**Moo!**
ISBN 978 0 7496 5332 3

**Izzie's Idea**
ISBN 978 0 7496 5334 7

**Roly-poly Rice Ball**
ISBN 978 0 7496 5333 0

**I Can't Stand It!**
ISBN 978 0 7496 5765 9

**Cockerel's Big Egg**
ISBN 978 0 7496 5767 3

**How to Teach a Dragon Manners**
ISBN 978 0 7496 5873 1

**The Truth about those Billy Goats**
ISBN 978 0 7496 5766 6

**Marlowe's Mum and the Tree House**
ISBN 978 0 7496 5874 8

**The Truth about Hansel and Gretel**
ISBN 978 0 7496 4708 7

**The Best Den Ever**
ISBN 978 0 7496 5876 2

**ADVENTURES**

**Aladdin and the Lamp**
ISBN 978 0 7496 6692 7

**Blackbeard the Pirate**
ISBN 978 0 7496 6690 3

**George and the Dragon**
ISBN 978 0 7496 6691 0

**Jack the Giant-Killer**
ISBN 978 0 7496 6693 4

**TALES OF KING ARTHUR**

**1. The Sword in the Stone**
ISBN 978 0 7496 6694 1

**2. Arthur the King**
ISBN 978 0 7496 6695 8

**3. The Round Table**
ISBN 978 0 7496 6697 2

**4. Sir Lancelot and the Ice Castle**
ISBN 978 0 7496 6698 9

**TALES OF ROBIN HOOD**

**Robin and the Knight**
ISBN 978 0 7496 6699 6

**Robin and the Monk**
ISBN 978 0 7496 6700 9

**Robin and the Silver Arrow**
ISBN 978 0 7496 6703 0

**Robin and the Friar**
ISBN 978 0 7496 6702 3

**FAIRY TALES**

**The Emperor's New Clothes**
ISBN 978 0 7496 7421 2

**Cinderella**
ISBN 978 0 7496 7417 5

**Snow White**
ISBN 978 0 7496 7418 2

**Jack and the Beanstalk**
ISBN 978 0 7496 7422 9

**The Three Billy Goats Gruff**
ISBN 978 0 7496 7420 5

**The Pied Piper of Hamelin**
ISBN 978 0 7496 7419 9

**Goldilocks and the Three Bears**
ISBN 978 0 7496 7897 5 *
ISBN 978 0 7496 7903 3

**Hansel and Gretel**
ISBN 978 0 7496 7898 2 *
ISBN 978 0 7496 7904 0

**The Three Little Pigs**
ISBN 978 0 7496 7899 9 *
ISBN 978 0 7496 7905 7

**Rapunzel**
ISBN 978 0 7496 7900 2 *
ISBN 978 0 7496 7906 4

**Little Red Riding Hood**
ISBN 978 0 7496 7901 9 *
ISBN 978 0 7496 7907 1

**Rumpelstiltskin**
ISBN 978 0 7496 7902 6*
ISBN 978 0 7496 7908 8

**Also look out for Hopscotch Histories and Hopscotch Myths!**

**\* hardback**